Toot Toot!

This book belongs to:

....

Down on the farm

the cockerel is **crowing**.

Cock-a-
doodle-doo

Tractor Ted is awake...

...but where is he going?

Over the field

full of cows **eating** grass.

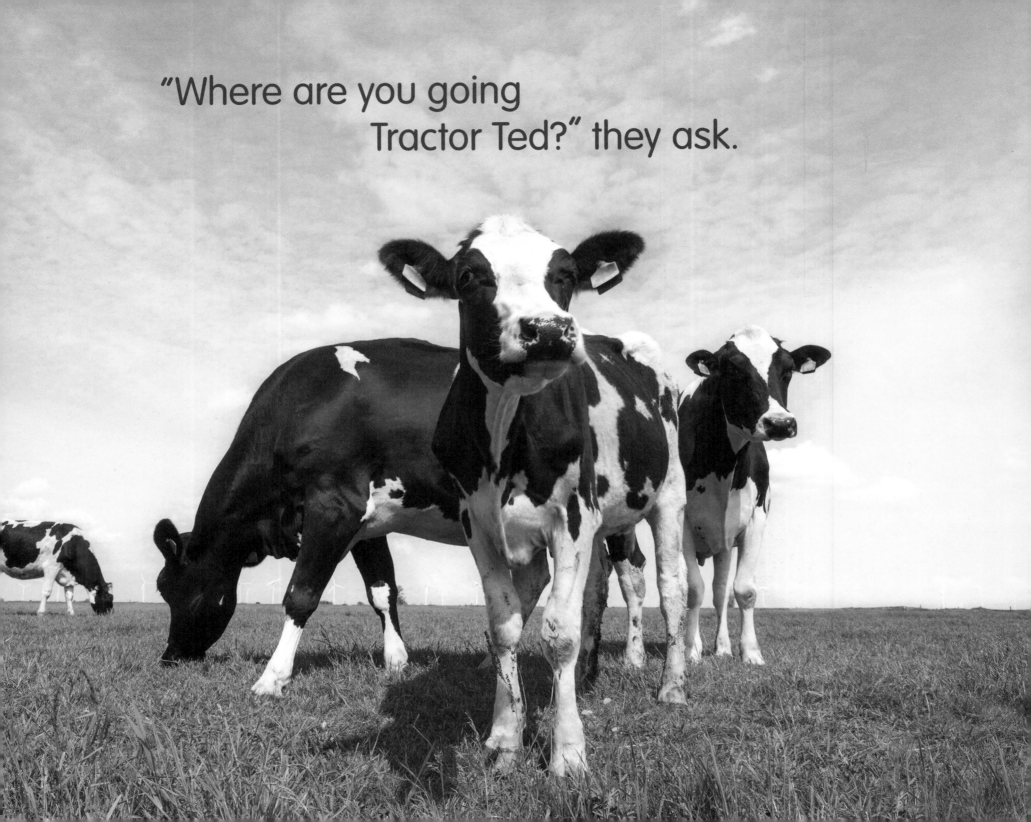

"Toot toot!"
he says, as he **passes** by...

Toot!
Toot!

He **drives** on past the tractors...

as they **plough**...

and they **mow**.

Past the huge
yellow combine

harvesting wheat.

He **drives** down past the barn
and then he can see
who he's been **looking** for.

Toot!
Toot!

Who can it be?

"Toot toot!"
    he says, as he **passes** by...

Ha ha! It is Midge the dog, that's who.

Tractor Ted says to her, "I've finally found you!"

"Toot toot!" he says,
as they both pass by!

Toot!
Toot!

TED 1